MRS. R...

and the Treasure Hunt

Robin Jones Gunn
Illustrated by Bill Duca

"God's laws are pure, eternal,
just. They are more desirable
than gold. They are sweeter
than honey dripping from a
honeycomb."
Psalm 19:9, 10 (TLB)

Chariot Books™
David C Cook Publishing Co.

For my own son, Ross Gunn IV,
and his good buddies, Jacob and Adam Hendrix
R.J.G.

To my second grade teacher, Kathleen Nelson,
for enough encouragement to last a lifetime
B.D.

Chariot Books™ is an imprint of David C. Cook Publishing Co.
David C. Cook Publishing Co., Elgin, Illinois 60120
David C. Cook Publishing Co., Weston, Ontario

MRS. ROSEY-POSEY AND THE TREASURE HUNT
©1991 by Robin Jones Gunn for text and Bill Duca for illustrations

Designed by Donna Kae Nelson
First Printing, 1991
Printed in Singapore
95 94 93 92 91 5 4 3 2 1

Library of Congress Cataloging-in-Publication Data
Gunn, Robin Jones
      Mrs. Rosey-Posey and the treasure hunt/ Robin Jones Gunn; illustrated by Bill
Duca.
         p.   cm. — (On my own books)
      Summary: A treasure hunt in and around Mrs. Rosey-Posey's house leads
Ross, Jacob, and Adam to their own copies of the Bible, the greatest treasure of all
time.
      ISBN 1-55513-372-X
      [1. Buried treasure--Fiction. 2. Bible--Fiction. 3. Christian Life--Fiction.]
I. Duca, Bill, ill. II. Title. III. Series: On my own books (Elgin, Ill.)
PZ7.G972Mr 1990
[E]--dc20   89-25244
                                                                          CIP
                                                                          AC

The verses marked (TLB) are taken from The Living Bible ©1971, owned by
assignment by the Illinois Regional Bank N.A. (as trustee). Used by permission of
Tyndale House Publishers Inc., Wheaton, IL 60189. All rights reserved.

Poppyville

When the sky is clear, and the air is warm, young boys dream of great adventure. And that is when the boys in Poppyville head straight for Mrs. Rosey-Posey's house.

One such day, Ross, Jacob, and Adam dressed like pirates and climbed into Mrs. Rosey-Posey's tree house. Jacob kept a lookout while Ross and Adam raised the flag.

"Captain, Captain!" Jacob cried. "Ship approaching! Starboard!"

Ross looked to the right. (That is the starboard side, you know.) He saw Mrs. Rosey-Posey pulling a little red wagon. She stopped in front of the tree house and called out, "Ahoy, Matey!"

"Who goes there?" called Ross.

" 'Tis I, your servant, Mrs. Rosey-Posey, with your daily ration of books and peaches."

"Very good," said Captain Ross. "Send them aboard."

Mrs. Rosey-Posey put the books and peaches in the bucket and pulled on the rope. Jacob grabbed the bucket and dumped out the cargo.

"Thank ye kindly," said Ross.

"Ye are most kindly welcome, Captain," said Mrs. Rosey-Posey. "If ye have further need of me, I shall be in the galley."

"She means the kitchen," said Ross.

"I know," said Jacob.

Adam rubbed his peach on his shirt. It helped get rid of the fuzz. Then he opened his book, and something fell out.

"Hey!" Adam said suddenly. "Look what I found in my book!"

"What is it?" Jacob asked.

The three boys looked closely at the
crumpled piece of paper.

"It's a secret treasure map!" Ross said.

"Wow!" said Adam.

"Are you sure?" said Jacob.

"Yes, look!" Ross said. "Here is the tree house. The arrows point to the porch swing."

"Then let's go!" said Jacob. "Let's find the treasure!"

The three pirates scrambled down the ladder and ran to the porch swing.

"Now where?" Jacob asked.

Ross turned the map sideways. "It looks like we go to the pond."

The boys ran to the pond.

"Now the arrows point to the house," said Jacob.

The boys raced up the steps to the back door.

"Now where?" Adam asked.

"I'm not sure," Ross said. He held the map close to have a better look.

"Hey! Somebody wrote something on the back!" Adam shouted.

Ross turned the map over and read,

"A treasure sweet

Like no other

Open it up

Adventures discover."

"What does that mean?" said Adam.

"A treasure sweet," Jacob said. "That must mean that the treasure is something to eat!"

Just then, Mrs. Rosey-Posey opened the back door. "Why, if it isn't my favorite pirates! Welcome! What brings ye to my galley?"

"We found a map," Ross said.

"A treasure map," Jacob added.

"It led us here, but we don't know where to go next," Adam told her.

"Indeed," said Mrs. Rosey-Posey. "May I have a look?"

Mrs. Rosey-Posey turned the map this way and that way. "Aye," she said. "This is a treasure map indeed. I believe it 'tis the other half of this one." She pulled another map from her pocket and handed it to the boys.

"Look!" Jacob cried. " 'X' marks the spot! But where do we start?"

"I believe ye boys start in the living room," Mrs. Rosey-Posey said.

They ran to the living room. "Now where? Now where?" Adam cried.

"Follow me!" Ross shouted.

The boys followed Ross through the
living room, into the dining room.
"Okay," Ross said, looking at the map, "I
think we go upstairs now."

"Come on, Matey," Jacob called to
Adam. "The treasure can't be far off!"

Adam hurried to catch up.

He found Ross and Jacob upstairs in a bedroom. They were going into a closet. "Wait for me!" Adam said.

The three of them pushed on the back of the closet wall. It opened into an empty closet in the next bedroom.

They laughed and ran out of the bedroom, into the hallway. "Look for a small door," Ross called over his shoulder.

There in the hallway, next to a small, open door, stood Mrs. Rosey-Posey. "Mercy me!" she exclaimed. "Does the treasure map say ye should go down my laundry chute?"

"I think so. That's the only small door in your hallway," said Ross.

"That's a laundry chute?" said Adam. "I've never seen a laundry chute like that before."

"Aye, Matey. My laundry chute is a one-of-a-kind." said Mrs. Rosey-Posey. "Ye best follow the map. Here. Use these."

She handed each of the pirates a laundry sack.

Captain Ross was the first one to slide down the long, dark laundry chute. "Wheee!" he cried as he landed in a pile of towels in the basement.

"Come on!" he called up to his friends. "It's really fun!"

Jacob went next, then Adam. They laughed all the way down.

"We must be getting close," Ross said, studying the map with a flashlight. "Look for a door that leads outside."

"Here it is!" cried Jacob. The pirates climbed out into the sunshine.

"Now we go twenty paces to the west," Ross said.

They looked at the weather vane on the top of Mrs. Rosey-Posey's house. The big "W" pointed straight toward the sandbox. Off they went, counting their paces: one, two, three. . . .

They stopped in front of a big "X" in the sand. "Come on!" they shouted and began to dig with all their might.

"This is it!" Ross cried. He and Jacob lifted an old treasure chest from the sand. Quickly, they opened it up.

The boys looked at the treasure. They looked at each other. Then they looked at the treasure again.

"What are they?" Jacob asked.

"What should we do with them?" Adam said.

Ross reached into the chest and took out
the three treasures. They looked like
books, but they were covered with
whipped cream.

"A treasure sweet!" said Ross. "Let's eat
them!" They all laughed and began
licking the whipped cream off the books.

Adam got whipped cream all over his
face. Jacob licked around the edges.

Ross licked the middle of his book.
Some letters began to appear—B-I-B-L . . .

"Look!" Ross shouted. "It's a Bible inside a plastic bag!"

"Really?" said Jacob. He kept licking to see if his treasure was a Bible, too.

"Let's go show Mrs. Rosey-Posey," Adam said. He had whipped cream everywhere.

"Mercy me!" cried Mrs. Rosey-Posey. "You've discovered the greatest treasure of all time! The Bible!"

She got that twinkle-sparkle-zing look in her eyes and said, "Did you know that the Bible is like a treasure map for our lives? If we follow the clues God left in His Word, and stay on His path, we will find a treasure better than gold."

"I never had my own Bible before,"
Adam said. "Thank you."

"Ye are most kindly welcome, Matey,"
said Mrs. Rosey-Posey. "These Bibles are
for each of you to keep for always."

"Why did you put whipped cream on
them?" Jacob asked.

"Thousands of years ago, there were teachers called 'rabbis.' They taught God's Word to young boys. First they would write a Bible verse on a clay tablet. Then they poured honey over it. The boys would lick off the honey and learn the Bible verse."

"I like whipped cream better than honey," said Adam.

"I thought you might," said Mrs. Rosey-Posey.

"Could you teach us some Bible verses?" asked Ross.

"I was hoping you would ask. I have just the ones for today!" said Mrs. Rosey-Posey. She helped each of the boys find Psalm 19 and read verse nine to them, "God's laws are pure, eternal, just."

The pirates repeated, "God's laws are pure, eternal, just."

"Did I just memorize a whole verse?" asked Adam.

"Indeed you did," said Mrs. Rosey-Posey.

Jacob read the next verse, "They are more desirable than gold." He stopped. "You mean the Bible is better than gold?"

"Indeed!" exclaimed Mrs. Rosey-Posey. "God's Word is going to last forever."

Ross read the rest of the verse. " 'They are sweeter than honey dripping from a honeycomb.' Hey, that's just like the clue, 'A treasure sweet.' "

"But what does the rest of the clue mean?" asked Jacob. He read the back of the map, "A treasure sweet, like no other, open it up, adventure discover."

Mrs. Rosey-Posey took Ross's Bible and held it like a special treasure. "The Bible is like no other book," she said. "When you open it up, you will see that it is full of adventure."

"It is?" said Adam.

"Indeed! The Bible is full of stories about giants and kings and warriors."

"Really?" said Adam.

Mrs. Rosey-Posey smiled and leaned forward. "It even has a true story about a donkey that talked."

"Wow!" said Jacob.

"One of my favorites," said Mrs. Rosey-Posey, "is a story about Paul. You see, first, he was shipwrecked on an island, and then he was bitten by a poisonous snake!"

"Then what happened?" Ross asked.

"Well, Matey, let's find out!" Mrs. Rosey-Posey said. She opened up to the book of Acts, chapter 27.

"Will you read about the talking donkey next?" Jacob asked.

"And then the story about the giant!" Adam said.

"Certainly," said Mrs. Rosey-Posey with a smile. "If ye Maties like these stories, just wait until ye hear some of the stories Jesus told His friends."

"First the shipwreck story," said Ross.

"Then the donkey!" said Adam.

Mrs. Rosey-Posey laughed and began to read. The three pirates stretched out. And of course, they all lifted their eye patches. It helped them to hear much better, you know.